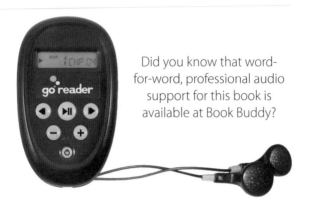

Did you know that word-for-word, professional audio support for this book is available at Book Buddy?

GoReader™ powered by Book Buddy is pre-loaded with word-for-word audio support to build strong readers and achieve Common Core standards.

The corresponding GoReader™ for this book can be found at: http://bookbuddyaudio.com

Or send an email to: info@bookbuddyaudio.com

BROADWAY JOE

A MAGIC LOCKER ADVENTURE

PETE BIRLE

Broadway Joe
A Magic Locker Adventure

Scobre Educational
2255 Calle Clara
La Jolla, CA 92037

Scobre Operations & Administration
42982 Osgood Road
Fremont, CA 94539

www.scobre.com
info@scobre.com

Scobre Educational publications may be purchased for
educational, business, or sales promotional use.

Cover and layout design by Jana Ramsay
Copyedited by Renae Reed

ISBN: 978-1-62920-122-1 (Soft Cover)
ISBN: 978-1-62920-121-4 (Library Bound)
ISBN: 978-1-62920-120-7 (eBook)

TABLE OF CONTENTS

1
LOWER END

Juanito pushed his way past MJ and exited the locker. "What is that smell?" he asked, wrinkling his nose.

"Beats me," said Jamie, right behind him. "But the air smells bad."

"It tastes worse," said MJ, pulling on his tongue with his thumb and forefinger, trying to get out whatever it was that had just landed in his mouth. "My mom probably made my favorite dinner, too, and is waiting for me by the back door," he added, shaking his head.

"Will you relax, dude?" Juanito said. "We're on another adventure here."

"Yeah, MJ," said Jamie. "Just try to enjoy the ride."

As MJ nodded, Juanito caught what had landed on MJ's tongue in the palm of his hand.

"What is this?" he asked, cradling one of the little black flakes that had fallen from the sky.

"It's ash," said the Coach, who joined them outside the locker.

"Do you think there's a volcano erupting?" asked MJ, shaking several flakes of ash from his hair.

"I doubt it," said the Coach. "More likely it's coming from those smokestacks over there."

The children looked off in the direction the Coach was pointing to see several smokestacks on the skyline atop the hills that surrounded them. The trees showed off every color; autumn was in full bloom. And, yet, because of the falling soot, the picture wasn't all that pretty. Everything seemed dark and damp.

"Where are we?" asked Juanito, trying to dodge the ash.

"Why don't you find out?" asked the Coach before walking back into the locker and disappearing.

The time travelers had landed in an alley next to the Babcock & Wilcox Company mill. According to the sign on the side of the building, the mill made steel tubing. No one would notice the locker up against the wall of the factory, MJ concluded. So, after they pushed it there, the children grabbed three University of Pittsburgh sweatshirts that had miraculously appeared in the locker and headed down the street.

Eventually, they came upon a bar, one of many on the block.

Standing inside the doorway was a man. A big man, with an unlit cigar wedged between his teeth.

"Excuse me, sir, what town is this?" asked Juanito.

"You mean you don't know where you are?" asked the man.

"We're from out of town," said Jamie quickly.

"You're in Beaver Falls, Pennsylvania," said the man. "Heaven on Earth, wouldn't you say?"

He then turned and entered the bar, leaving the children on the street.

"Beaver Falls," said MJ. "What's so special about this place?"

"I don't know," said Jamie. "But now that we know *where* we are, let's find out *when*. . . ."

The kids started walking down Fifth Street, passing bar after bar. While there was some activity downtown, it was generally quiet. It seemed that everyone was either at home or inside one of those factories up on the hill.

The cars parked on the street, however, indicated that they had indeed gone back in time. The Studebaker coupes, Buick sedans, and Ford paneled wagons spoke of days long gone. The low $5,500 price tag on the brand-new Cadillac Fleetwood in the dealership lot confirmed it.

Eventually, the children found themselves around the corner, on Sixth Street, in a neighborhood of two-story frame houses. On one side was the Beaver River, and on the other was Pennsylvania Railroad.

"If you boys are looking for the game with the Lower End gang, head on over to the Harmony Dwellings," said an African-American woman, who was walking by with another black lady. The one who spoke stopped and looked the three youngsters up and down. She focused particularly on the white girl standing in front of her.

"Good luck, young lady," she said, chuckling a bit to herself as she addressed Jamie. "You may shortly wish you had stayed on the other side of the tracks."

"Yes," said the other woman, herself giggling. "Life is a lot easier up there in Patterson Heights."

The three kids looked at each other and shrugged, not knowing what the ladies were talking about.

They soon found out. Upon arriving at the Harmony Dwellings, a housing project, they walked into a pickup football game in progress on a homemade field.

"Well, lookie here!" said a scrawny white kid, noticing the arrival of the three friends from the future. "My fans have arrived to see me whup you Hilltop Boys."

The boy with the over-confident attitude was playing quarterback. No older than Jamie, MJ or Juanito, he was the only white kid on an all-black team, and the only one with a helmet, shoulder pads, and football pants.

"We'll give you the three new kids," said one of the Hilltop Boys to the quarterback. "Even the girl."

"We'll take 'em," said the boy with a smirk. "And then we'll beat you."

The three friends from the future walked over to join the game.

"Are you any good?" asked the quarterback. "To

play with me, you got to be good."

Remembering what the locker could do for their athletic abilities, Jamie responded with a grin, "Yeah, we're good."

"Ok, then. Let's get to it," the boy said. "You three can sub in and out every few plays."

Once on the field, the time travelers showed off their skills, and it wasn't long before they were on the field for every down. They ran, blocked, caught the ball, and tackled like all-pros. MJ caught several touchdown passes, Juanito had a pair of interceptions that he ran back for touchdowns ("pick sixes"), and Jamie brought down every boy that foolishly tried to put a move on her. But, it wasn't that easy to focus on the game when they couldn't take their eyes off their quarterback. Although he could barely see over center, he was clearly the best player on the field. Calling out plays, he ran his offense like a seasoned veteran.

More impressive, though, was his ability to throw the ball. He already knew how to grip it correctly. He threw the ball the right way, not winding up but letting it go from his ear. He got rid of it fast, too, showing a quick release.

Jamie, MJ, and Juanito wondered if he had a magic locker, too!

After the Lower End team—and its pint-sized yet overly confident QB—beat up on the Hilltop Boys, the players began to leave. Passing by Jamie, MJ, and Juanito was Linwood, one of their teammates.. At that very point, Linwood turned around and said, "Thanks to these three and to you, Joe Willie, we beat those rich kids from up in the hills . . . and we beat 'em bad."

Then he shouted, so everyone within earshot could hear, "We're the sandlot champs of 1952!"

Jamie was trying to put it all together in her head. She was deep in thought. Within a few seconds, a smile came over her face. As the rest of the children disappeared, including the quarterback named Joe, Jamie grabbed her friends by their arms.

"C'mon," she said excitedly. "Let's get back to the locker. I think I know why we're here."

2
GREATNESS
IN THE MAKING

"Joe Namath!" yelled MJ, as the three made their way back to Fifth Street and the locker. "Are you sure?"

"She should be," said the Coach, who once again appeared out of nowhere. "That was Joe Namath."

"Wow!" said Juanito. "We played football with Joe Namath when he was a kid."

Juanito then paused, the look of amazement gone from his face. "Who's Joe Namath?" he asked.

The Coach chuckled. "Only one of the best

quarterbacks of all time," he said.

"He sure was awesome today," said MJ, shaking his head. "I wish I could throw the ball like he can."

"That little dude is one of the best ever?" asked Juanito, finding it hard to believe. "I'm almost bigger than him."

The kids walked for a few minutes, recalling every detail of what they were just a part of.

"Hey Jamie, you said you thought you knew why we were here, not who the quarterback was," MJ said. "What do you think we need to do for Joe Namath?"

"He looks like he doesn't need any help . . . from anyone."

"I don't really know yet," said Jamie, looking over at the Coach. "But I'm pretty sure we'll find out once we get back in the locker, don't you think?"

The Coach winked.

"Well, what are we waiting for?" said Juanito.

After the locker stopped shaking, the light went away and the door swung open. Immediately, the children noticed they were right back where they started, in the alley next to the Babcock & Wilcox mill in Beaver Falls, Pennsylvania.

"We didn't go anywhere," said Juanito. "That's never happened before."

"Maybe we didn't go some*place*, but by the looks of Fifth Street, we definitely went some*time*," said MJ.

The cars had changed; the updated Cadillac Fleetwood now went for $9,500. And the men, women, and children wore more modern clothing as they made their way down the street. The streets were packed with people. Everyone—kids and adults—seemed to be in a hurry, heading off in the same direction.

Once again, it was Juanito who approached one of them.

"Excuse me, but where is everyone going?" he asked.

"Where have *you* been, kid?" responded a man. He was nearly jogging, his two little girls trying to keep up. "We're trying to get over to Reeves Stadium before kickoff. Don't you know that Joey U can end a high school football game almost before it starts?"

The kids, without missing a beat, got in line and started following the crowd.

"I bet we're going to see Joe Namath play high school football," said MJ.

"I wonder if he'll be as good as he is in all those old NFL highlight films I've seen," said Jamie.

"He'll probably be better," said Juanito.

"Keep your eyes and ears open," Jamie reminded the others. "We still don't know exactly why we're here."

Her pals nodded. Shortly, they arrived at the field. Magically, Jamie suddenly had enough money for them to buy tickets. It's a good thing, too, since the game was a sellout. They luckily found three seats near the 30-yard line on the home Tigers' side of the field.

It was 1960, Joe Namath's senior year at Beaver Falls. From the conversations of those heading toward the game, the town belonged to Namath—who was referred to as "Joey U," in honor of his hero, Baltimore Colts quarterback Johnny Unitas.

Like "Johnny U," Namath wore Number 19. The boys spotted him immediately on the field at Geneva College, where Beaver Falls played its home games.

He was still small, and yet he stood out again—not so much for his lack of size as he did for his attitude. He displayed a confidence that inflated his little body. It was the way he carried himself. Like he knew things everyone else on the field didn't. He was . . . cool.

The man sitting next to the three youngsters seemed to take delight in the fact that they were pointing and talking about the pint-sized quarterback for the Beaver Falls Tigers. He introduced himself to them as John Namath, the QB's father.

"I see all Joey's games," he said proudly. "I even watch his practices."

The children wondered if he dressed up for his son's workouts, too. Sitting next to them, John Namath wore a freshly pressed suit—a white suit, no less. On his feet were shiny, two-toned saddle shoes. He didn't fit in among all the mill workers who filled the stands, wearing their overalls and boots.

The kids thought that wearing a white suit in Beaver Falls, with all the furnaces spitting out soot, was odd. But he did look good. They had to give him that. Maybe Joe got some of his confidence from his dad, they whispered to one another.

Turns out that John Namath was, in fact, a factory employee. He told the children that he worked daily at Babcock & Wilcox, the same mill next to the alley where the kids had hidden the locker.

"Last week, 7,000 people showed up to listen to presidential candidate John F. Kennedy talk on the steps of City Hall," Namath said to the boys. "But a whole lot more showed up to see my boy beat Farrell. This is Beaver Falls' year. One more victory next week, against Ellwood City, plus a loss by Monessen, and we'll be Western Pennsylvania champs."

By the looks of what Jamie, MJ, and Juanito saw on the field that day, the result was a sure thing. "Joey U" Namath was 13 for 17 for 232 yards as his Tigers beat Aliquippa easily, 34-7.

But the stats only told half the story. What the kids witnessed that night was a football superstar in the making. Joe Namath, although only in high school, was the real deal.

Jamie, MJ, and Juanito were amazed at the young athlete's ability to vary the speed of his passes and throw from different angles. Namath would loop one pass and bullet another. While the opposing QB was struggling to just throw it the same way each time, Joe was fine-tuning his already advanced skills.

Not only was he demonstrating his knowledge of throwing, but he was showing off his ball skills, too. Hiding the pigskin inside two of the biggest hands the kids had ever seen on a teenager, Joe often left the opposing defenders scratching their heads. They'd be piled on top of one of Beaver Falls' running backs—

unaware that Joe still had the ball and was heading downfield.

Suddenly, the Coach appeared and sat down on the stadium steps next to the children. No one but the kids could see or hear him.

"Even more impressive," he said, "was the fact that Joe called his own game, showing off his knowledge of football's finer points."

"What do you mean by 'called his own game?'" asked Juanito.

"Joe picked all the plays in the huddle and called all the audibles—the last-second changes in plays—at the line of scrimmage, not his coach."

The kids were quite impressed. And then, before the gun sounded to end the game, Joe gave Jamie, MJ, and Juanito a look at his specialty.

It was called the "jump pass," which Joe would throw after his feet had already left the ground. When that happened, they got a good look at his cleats. Namath's shoes weren't the popular high-tops of the era, which afforded better ankle support. Joe opted for a low-cut style—much "cooler," the kids determined.

"I remember the first time Coach Bruno played Joe at quarterback," said his father, as the crowd made its way down out of the bleachers. "It was against New Brighton for the mud jug, a symbol of bragging rights. Joe came on in the second quarter with Beaver Falls already up 14-0. His first pass was a 24-yard TD toss, one of three touchdown passes he'd throw that day.

"Let's just say I knew right then he was going to be a special player."

The children shook John Namath's hand before saying good-bye and making their way back to the locker.

As they walked past a bunch of high school students, they couldn't help but overhear a boy. He looked a lot like the kid everyone called Linwood from the sandlot game, only older.

"Most competitive kid I ever met," said Linwood. "You knock him down, he gets right back up.

"Joe isn't a pretty boy," he added. "And we always knew he was a quarterback. We knew before anybody."

The three time travelers knew it, too.

"This guy's got it all together," said MJ. "What does he need us for?"

"Yeah," said Juanito. "What could we possibly do to help Joe Namath?"

"I don't know," said Jamie, shaking her head. "But there must be something."

3
ROLL TIDE

The locker door opened to some hot and steamy weather.

"This feels like we're back in the South again," said Juanito, poking his head out of the locker.

"We are," said MJ. "Look!"

Jamie and Juanito turned to see what their friend was pointing at. There, right in front of them, was a banner hanging on the side of a building. It said in big, bright, red letters "Welcome freshman football players to Tuscaloosa, home of the University of Alabama

Crimson Tide."

The children tiptoed out of the locker. It was early morning, and apparently no one on campus was awake yet.

The locker had landed on the steps of Paul W. Bryant Hall, a majestic brick building with four white columns in front. After moving the locker around to the side and hiding it behind a couple of bushes, the kids tried the front door.

To their surprise, it was open.

Once inside, they went exploring. They quickly determined they were in a dormitory that housed the Alabama Crimson Tide football team. Notices on the walls told the residents when they had to be at practice, when they could eat lunch, when they should be lifting weights, when they should be studying, and when it was time to go to bed.

"Why do you think we came here?" whispered Juanito. "Did Joe Namath play at Alabama?"

"He sure did," said MJ, who was at that moment

paging through a copy of a 1965 Alabama football media guide he had picked up off a coffee table.

"Listen to this," he said, trying hard not to get so excited that his voice might wake someone. "Joe Namath was one of the best college quarterbacks ever."

Jamie and Juanito moved closer to hear. MJ began reading:

"*In his first game on Sept. 22, 1962, Namath threw three touchdown passes, tying a school record.*

"*Still, Coach Bryant brought him along slowly.*"

"Did you say 'Coach Bryant?'" asked Jamie. "I wonder if this dorm is named after him."

"I guess it is," said MJ, turning to another page. "It says here the longtime coach of Alabama is Paul W. 'Bear' Bryant."

"Read some more about Joe Namath," said Juanito.

MJ went back to the page he was on before and continued reading:

"*Namath seemed to stretch the field. As a*

sophomore, he broke school records for passing yardage (1,192) and completions (76), while tying the marks for touchdown passes in a season (13).

"His junior year saw him mature even more as field general. With Bryant realizing that a quarterback's true talent lies in his head and not his arm, the coach even used Namath on defense, as a safety, to take advantage of his ability to read the angles on both sides of the ball.

"He just completed his senior year, in which Namath established himself as Alabama's career leader in touchdown passes by the third game of the Tide's 1964 national championship season."

MJ stopped for a second. "Here's the best part," he said.

"'This boy is great,' said Bear Bryant. 'If he doesn't sign one of the biggest professional contracts ever, I'll be awfully surprised.'"

"Did he?" asked Juanito.

"Yes, he did," said the Coach. "Signing that

contract and then playing for the New York Jets meant more for the business of professional football than many realize."

Just then, the children heard a series of alarm clocks go off, one after the other. Panicked that the Alabama football players might find them, they took off for the door.

Once outside, Juanito said, "Maybe we're supposed to stay here."

"I don't think so," Jamie said. "Namath's college career is already over, and it sounds like he didn't need any help."

"So, where are we headed now?" asked MJ, as the three kids started to jog.

"My . . . guess is," Jamie said between breaths, "we're headed . . . for New York."

4
THE CITY
THAT NEVER SLEEPS

As the kids hurtled through time and space, the Coach gave them a history lesson.

Eleven names were called out before the St. Louis Cardinals selected Joe Namath with the 12th pick of the 1965 National Football League Draft.

Perhaps Joe Willie was insulted. If he was, he never said anything. He just waited. Shortly thereafter, another team also drafted him: the New York Jets of the rival American Football League. The Jets, and their hall-of-fame owner Sonny Werblin, put their money where their mouths were. They signed Namath for a reported $427,000. It was the kind of salary that was unheard of back then.

It was also the AFL's biggest victory to date in its inter-league war with the established NFL. And it was what paved the way for the leagues to eventually merge.

In the meantime, though, Joe Namath was heading to the Big Apple. It seemed like the stars had lined up perfectly.

"Back then," said the Coach, "the NFL ruled professional football. At the time, a lot of people thought the AFL was inferior, like the minor leagues in baseball.

"The night before the Jets played the Colts in Super Bowl III, one NFL coach was asked what he thought of Namath," the Coach continued. "He said he'd have to wait until Sunday night, after Joe had played his first pro game—even though he had already been in the AFL four years."

"So, after just a few years in the league, Joe took the Jets to the Super Bowl?" asked Juanito.

"And then the AFL and NFL merged, right?" asked MJ.

"Yes and yes," said the Coach before disappearing again once the locker touched down.

Immediately, the kids realized where they were. They half expected it, in fact. They were in Shea Stadium, in the borough of Queens, New York. The year was 1968 and, by the looks of the Jets' locker room, something special had just happened there.

The kids were alone, though; everyone who had been there earlier that day was gone. But they left clues about their celebration, in the form of empty champagne bottles.

Someone had forgotten to turn off a TV that was hanging from the ceiling in one corner of the locker room. The children looked at the screen. On it was a news report about Joe Namath, now known as "Broadway Joe." There he was on the sidelines of a

Jets' game, in a full-length fur coat, sporting the same boldness and confidence he displayed as a kid in the Lower End. The announcer was talking about how Namath was the first pro quarterback to pass for 4,000 yards, which he did in 1967.

On the floor was a stat sheet, most likely left behind by a reporter. Juanito picked it up and showed it to his friends.

It indicated that the Jets had just defeated the Oakland Raiders, 27-23, before 62,627 fans, in the AFL Championship Game. Quarterback Joe Namath sparked a fourth quarter come-from-behind victory over the defending champs by tossing the last of three TD passes.

Just then, a voice on the TV finished the story that the stat sheet told. The Jets, as a result of the victory, would represent the AFL in Super Bowl III in Miami.

Jamie went over and turned off the TV, just in case someone could hear it.

"You know," the Coach said, stepping outside the

locker, "the first two Super Bowls were dominated by the NFL's Green Bay Packers and Coach Vince Lombardi.

"And in Super Bowl III, the Colts will be heavy favorites to crush the Jets—and the AFL."

"Do the Jets even have a chance?" asked Juanito.

"More than a chance," said the Coach. "Remember, they have Broadway Joe Namath."

"So what does he need us for?" asked MJ.

"Yeah," said Juanito, annoyed. "Why are we here?"

"Come on back inside the locker," said the Coach. "You'll know as soon as you speak to Joe."

As the children made their way back into the locker, MJ said something that caught his friends off-guard.

"This trip is not only an adventure, but an even bigger mystery than the last one," said MJ, for the first time not concerned about the ongoing time travel. "It's pretty cool."

Jamie and Juanito grinned, and even the Coach managed a smile.

5

THE GUARANTEE

Although the sun had already set, the heat of Miami hit the children as soon as the locker door opened.

Having landed in the middle of a grove of palm trees, the locker was well hidden. So, the kids took a look around. Across the street was a Cadillac dealership, where the price of a new Fleetwood was now more than $10,000. They learned they were just in time for the Miami Touchdown Club's annual presentation of its FAME award. According to the sign outside the fancy Miami Springs Villas, that night Joe

Namath was to receive the group's award for Player of the Year. It would be the first time the honor was given to someone from the AFL.

"We still don't know why we're here," said Jamie.

"So, then let's get in there," said Juanito, pointing to the front door.

"Why don't we go around back?" suggested MJ. "We don't want to be kicked out, and I sure don't want to miss any of this."

The youngsters made their way toward what looked like a service entrance to the private club where the dinner was being held. As they did, they noticed a man leaning up against a tree. Usually the picture of calm, cool, and collected, on this night, Joe Namath was not.

"That's him," whispered Juanito as the three friends approached.

"We know," Jamie and MJ responded.

Namath spotted the three kids heading his way.

"Hey," said Namath. "Out a little late tonight, aren't you?"

The wheels started turning in Jamie's head. "We came to see you," she answered. "To wish you luck."

"For my speech tonight or for Sunday's game?" asked Joe Willie.

"For both," said Juanito.

"How are you feeling about your chances against the Colts?" asked MJ.

"Well, you know, I believe everything I've said all week, how we're going to beat them, how people should bet the ranch on the Jets," said Namath. "I'm just being honest, like I always am.

"But I know it's rubbing a lot of people the wrong way," he added. "Maybe I should tone it down a bit, especially tonight."

"Why?" asked Jamie.

"I'm not really sure," Namath responded. "But I woke up last night feeling really weird, like something was wrong."

The jaws of all three children dropped open. They turned to each other with a look of understanding.

They now knew exactly what the Coach had meant when he said they needed to speak to Joe Namath. No longer was Namath sounding like the bold and arrogant quarterback they first met as a kid playing sandlot ball in Beaver Falls. He had lost his confidence, perhaps the one thing more than any other that had defined his life and career.

"NO!" all three yelled at once.

Namath looked surprised.

"I'm just saying maybe I should back off," he explained. "We're 17-point underdogs. The Colts were 13-1 in the regular season and demolished Cleveland, 34-0, in the NFL title game.

"Not only that," Namath continued, "but they have the top-rated defense in the league. They've allowed the fewest points in the history of the game. In fact, some folks think they might be the greatest team of all time."

Joe Namath turned to make his way back to the dinner, his head down.

The children knew it was now or never. They just had to speak up. Juanito ran ahead and grabbed Broadway Joe by the arm.

"Mr. Namath," he began, "you have to stick to your guns. You have to keep on telling the world how you think the Jets will beat the Colts. You can't back down now."

"I admire your spunk, kid," said Joe Willie, chuckling. "You remind me of . . . me."

"You don't know the half of it," said Jamie, rolling her eyes.

"But maybe I should just let us do what we need to do on the field, and leave the rest alone," Namath added. "Maybe a true champion should be humble and keep his mouth shut."

"But then, you wouldn't be Broadway Joe," said Juanito. "Then, you'd be just like everyone else. And you're certainly not like everyone else."

"Yeah," piped in Jamie. "It wasn't just your ability that brought you to this point in your career. It was your confidence, too. You can't turn your back on it now."

The quarterback looked long and hard at the three youngsters.

"You know, it was never bragging or boasting on my part," said Namath. "I've just always felt I could do what I said, back it up on the field, because of my confidence."

"And your teammates know that," said Jamie, the locker once again giving her reasoning beyond her years. "They're counting on you to be their leader. If you tone it down in your speech tonight, how do you think they'll respond? How do you think they'll play?"

Namath stared at Jamie, MJ, and Juanito for what seemed like forever, deep in thought.

"You kids are right," he finally said. "I need to be true to myself and my teammates. I mean, I'm Joe Namath!"

"And I'm Juanito," said the littlest time traveler, which made everyone laugh.

"Thanks for setting me straight, guys," said Namath. "C'mon. I'll sneak you guys into the back. You're Jets fans, aren't you?"

"Oh yes!" they said in unison as they followed Joe Namath inside.

Within minutes, Joe was called to the microphone to say a few words. He did, tossing out a few footballs to the crowd as well. It was then that a fan of the Colts shouted out what he thought was going to happen on Sunday. To which Joe responded, "The Jets will win Sunday. I guarantee it."

In the back of the room, Jamie, MJ, and Juanito gave each other high fives as the room got deathly quiet. Joe Namath had uttered the line that made all of sports take notice. Though he'd said before that he thought his team would win, Joe hadn't guaranteed anything until now. His guarantee was outrageous, soon to be the stuff of legend. Hearing it, they knew they had accomplished their mission. They turned and headed for the locker.

Stepping inside, they wondered if they'd be rewarded for helping Joe Namath display the pride that made him famous—with one final trip.

They weren't disappointed. The locker's next stop was an open maintenance closet on the upper deck of the Miami Orange Bowl, three days later, at the start of Super Bowl III.

6
SUPER BOWL III

Of course, Joe Namath's guarantee had become a topic of conversation the past several days.

By Sunday, January 12, 1969, it was front-page news. It certainly captured a lot of people's interest, long before it would become "The Guarantee," the most famous prediction since Babe Ruth's "Called Shot" home run in Game 3 of the 1932 World Series.

It was one of the reasons why, on Sunday, a capacity crowd of 75,377 was at the Orange Bowl to watch Joe Namath and his Jets face off against the

Colts. And it was why millions more were watching on TV.

Under that kind of spotlight, how could Namath not be . . . well, Namath? The day belonged to him, and he knew it from the get-go.

The brash 25-year-old quarterback was every bit as good as advertised—and much better than the Colts ever imagined. With his quick release, he beat Baltimore's blitz with snap passes, most of the time to split end George Sauer, who caught eight balls in all for 133 yards.

Namath directed the Jets' offense with patience and precision. He mixed up his passes with the powerful running of Matt Snell, who gained 121 yards and scored the Jets' lone TD.

At the half, it was 7-0 New York, and Earl Morrall, playing for the injured Johnny Unitas, had already been intercepted three times. As a result, Baltimore Coach Don Shula brought "Johnny U" off the bench in the third quarter with the Colts down, 13-0, to try to get something going. But it was too little, too late. The Jets were in such command by then that Namath's boyhood idol couldn't make up the ground. Joe Willie didn't even have to throw a pass in the fourth period. He just ran out the clock.

And when it was over, following one of sports' greatest upsets, Broadway Joe Namath trotted off the field wagging his right index finger in the air. As the three time travelers cheered, the flashbulbs went off like fireworks.

7
LARGER THAN LIFE

On their way back to the locker after the game, the Coach arrived to fill the kids in on the rest:

The Jets brought the AFL its first Super Bowl victory and the standing it needed for the two leagues to merge. Agreed upon in 1966, the union was finally completed in 1970.

But it was Joe Namath whose star power put the Super Bowl at the top of American sports. Today, the Super Bowl has surpassed the World Series, the Kentucky Derby, and the Indianapolis 500 as

America's number-one sporting event.

His numbers in the big game were not spectacular (17 completions in 28 attempts for 206 yards), but he was such a commanding figure that he was voted the game's Most Valuable Player. To this day, he's the only quarterback who did not toss at least one touchdown pass to be voted Super Bowl MVP.

Rightly so, he gave the game ball that his teammates awarded him to the AFL. Joe said it was a symbol of the league's coming of age in professional football.

Lastly, he convinced an entire generation of superstar athletes to boldly predict their team's dominance, spark a bit of controversy, and keep the fans talking.

"Remember what one reporter wrote about him," said the Coach. "'Joe Namath was a larger-than-life figure. At 21, he was a star. By the time he was 25, he was a legend.'"

The children had heard all they needed to know about Joe Namath. They broke into a trot on the way back to the locker, waving their index fingers in the air.

Once inside, the door closed, the locker began to shake, and a glow of light came through the air vents at the top. Then, just as suddenly, the locker stopped shaking, the light went away. . . .

"Think your mom is waiting for you?" Juanito asked MJ, as the door began to swing open.

"Maybe," said MJ with a smirk. "But I'd be okay with it if we don't land back in Jamie's garage."

"How do you feel about *here*?" Juanito asked, exiting the locker.

"Where's here?" asked Jamie.

"Beats me," said MJ, himself now outside. "But it looks like we're at the Super Bowl again."

Did you know that word-for-word, professional audio support for this book is available at Book Buddy?

GoReader™ powered by Book Buddy is pre-loaded with word-for-word audio support to build strong readers and achieve Common Core standards.

The corresponding GoReader™ for this book can be found at: http://bookbuddyaudio.com

Or send an email to: info@bookbuddyaudio.com